To Amanda, Caroline, Geralda, Hannah, Lyda, Rebecca, Susan, and Susan
—L. B.

In rosy-cozy memory of winter evenings with my mom
—H. N.

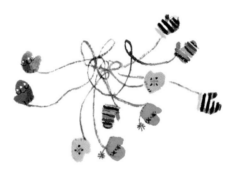

Henry Holt and Company, LLC, *Publishers since 1866*
115 West 18th Street, New York, New York 10011
www.henryholt.com

Henry Holt is a registered trademark of Henry Holt and Company, LLC
Text copyright © 2005 by Lynne Berry. Illustrations copyright © 2005 by Hiroe Nakata.
All rights reserved. Distributed in Canada by H. B. Fenn and Company Ltd.

Library of Congress Cataloging-in-Publication Data
Berry, Lynne. Duck skates / Lynne Berry; illustrated by Hiroe Nakata.—1st ed.
        p.   cm.
Summary: Five little ducks skate, romp, and play in the snow.
[1. Ducks—Fiction. 2. Snow—Fiction. 3. Stories in rhyme.] I. Nakata, Hiroe, ill. II. Title.
PZ8.3.B4593Du 2005   [E]—dc22   2004022176
ISBN-13: 978-0-8050-7219-8
ISBN-10: 0-8050-7219-5
First Edition—2005 / Designed by Hiroe Nakata and Donna Mark
Printed in the United States of America on acid-free paper. ∞
1 3 5 7 9 10 8 6 4 2

The artist used watercolor and ink to create the illustrations for this book.

Duck Skates

Lynne Berry

ILLUSTRATED BY Hiroe Nakata

HENRY HOLT AND COMPANY • NEW YORK

"Wake up! Wake up!" two ducks shout.
"Snow is falling! All ducks out!"

Two ducks run for their bright new boots,

Race for the snow in their new snowsuits.

The last three follow. All five tromp
Down to the pond for a duck-skate romp.

Five ducks toss ten boots in a jumble,

Lace up skates, and begin to stumble.

One duck wobbles.

Two ducks wiggle.

Three
ducks
topple.

Four ducks giggle.

Five little ducks now glide in line
Down by the bank to a NO-SKATE sign.

The sign says STOP!

The sign says SNOW!

Two ducks grin,

and the ducks all GO!

The first two lead with a duck-skate dash.

The last three chase—and the ducks all crash!

Five little ducks land deep in snow.
Three ducks duck when the first two THROW!

Snowballs zoom with a *zip-zap-zing*.
All five ducks now dodge and fling.
"Mercy! Mercy!" two ducks cry.
Three ducks cheer as the last balls fly.

Three ducks climb
from the deep snow pile.
Five little ducks shake hands
and smile.

Whish and *swish* and the ducks go round.

Ducks in a line skate homeward-bound.

Five ducks flop by the uphill track.

"Skates off! Boots on!" five ducks quack.

Five ducks tramp. Ten boots stamp.
Ducks trudge hungry, cold, and damp.

The first two stop at the top and peer.
"Hurry, ducks, now home is near!"

Three ducks slip down the hill and slide.
Two ducks, stomping, tromp inside.

Five ducks wrestle ten wet boots,

Hang damp mittens, skates, and suits.

Five little ducks dry ten duck feet. Rub down feathers.

Now ducks eat!

Cake and cocoa, milk and pie,
Five little ducks lick crumbs and sigh.
Ducks cuddle up on the round hearth rug,
Rosy, cozy, warm, and snug.